This book belongs to:

_____

I am VERY important to God!

CHRISTIAN

written
and illustrated by
Joan Hutson

Pauline

BOOKS & MEDIA

BOSTON

Library of Congress Cataloging-in-Publication Data

Hutson, Joan.
   Kristian / written and illustrated by Joan Hutson.
      p.   cm.
   Summary: Kristian makes the world a better place because she
   spends her day doing good deeds for others.
   ISBN 0-8198-4202-8
   [1. Christian life—Fiction.]   I. Title.
PZ7.H965Kr 1995
[E]—dc20   95-4316
                                             CIP
                                           AC

Printed and published in the U.S.A. by Pauline Books & Media,
50 St. Paul's Avenue, Boston, MA 02130.

Pauline Books & Media is the publishing house of the Daughters of
St. Paul, an international congregation of women religious serving the
Church with the communications media.

1 2 3 4 5   99 98 97 96 95

Kristian

Once upon a time there was Kristian.

She lived on a hill so high some said it touched the sky!

9

Kristian looked like an ordinary girl,
but she had an EXTRAORDINARY heart.

Every morning as the golden sun kissed
her awake, she prayed:

"Dear God, help me to be in the most
helpful places today so I can help as
many people as possible!"

God did not receive many prayers like that,
so He was glad to say, "YES."

13

Kristian did her loving deeds so quietly, gently, and lovingly that many times God was the only one who noticed all her kindness.

"KRISTIAN, KRISTIAN,
WHERE ARE YOU?"
"SCRUBBING,
SCRUBBING...IS A CLUE!"

"KRISTIAN, KRISTIAN,
WHERE ARE YOU?"
"SHARING,
SHARING...IS A CLUE!"

"KRISTIAN, KRISTIAN,
WHERE ARE YOU?"
"GATHERING,
GATHERING...IS A CLUE!"

"KRISTIAN, KRISTIAN,
WHERE ARE YOU?"
"HOLDING,
HOLDING...IS A CLUE!"

"KRISTIAN, KRISTIAN,
WHERE ARE YOU?"
"PULLING,
PULLING...IS A CLUE!"

"KRISTIAN, KRISTIAN,
WHERE ARE YOU?"
"FILLING,
FILLING...IS A CLUE!"

"KRISTIAN, KRISTIAN,
WHERE ARE YOU?"
"DRYING,
DRYING...IS A CLUE!"

29

"KRISTIAN, KRISTIAN,
WHERE ARE YOU?"
"LIFTING,
LIFTING...IS A CLUE!"

"KRISTIAN, KRISTIAN,
WHERE ARE YOU?"
"SUPPLYING,
SUPPLYING...IS A CLUE!"

"KRISTIAN, KRISTIAN,
WHERE ARE YOU?"
"PILING,
PILING...IS A CLUE!"

"KRISTIAN, KRISTIAN,
WHERE ARE YOU?"
"CARING,
CARING...IS A CLUE!"

"KRISTIAN, KRISTIAN,
WHERE ARE YOU?"
"LOVING,
LOVING...IS A CLUE!"

"KRISTIAN, KRISTIAN,
WHERE ARE YOU?"
"CELEBRATING,
CELEBRATING...IS A CLUE!"

41

Then one day the sun's kiss did not awaken Kristian. Instead she was carried away by a dream.

Angel choirs were singing wonderful melodies.

Suddenly she was surrounded by ALL the people she had helped during her lifetime. There were hundreds of people! Hundreds of smiling people! Old people, young people, short people, tall people, narrow people, wide people, quiet people and not so quiet people!

47

Then Kristian heard a beautiful Voice say:

"THANK YOU, KRISTIAN.
YOU HAVE MADE MY WORLD
A BETTER WORLD TO LIVE IN.
YOU *HAVE* HELPED AS MANY
PEOPLE AS POSSIBLE, AND
YOUR *GOOD DEEDS* WILL SHINE
FOREVER. THANK YOU!"

THANK YOU!

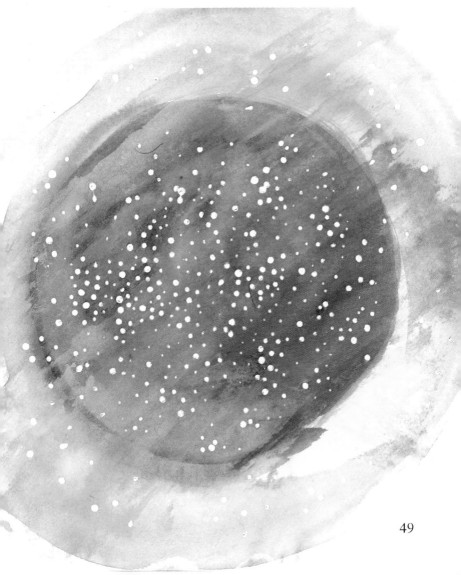

For you to do:

1. Make a little book by stapling together sheets of blank paper. Use your own name as the title. On the first pages, draw pictures of yourself doing different actions that are pleasing to God and to other people.

2. Next draw in pictures of people you have already helped in some way.

3. Pretend that God let you have a dream like Kristian's. On the last page of your book, draw a picture of what you saw in the dream.

4. Get a small pocket notebook. Write out a list of some Christian actions you can do. Keep your notebook with you. Every time you do one of these kind deeds, mark down the date beside it in your notebook.

Pauline BOOKS & MEDIA

ALASKA
750 West 5th Ave., Anchorage, AK
  99501; 907-272-8183
CALIFORNIA
3908 Sepulveda Blvd., Culver City, CA
  90230; 310-397-8676
5945 Balboa Ave., San Diego, CA
  92111; 619-565-9181
46 Geary Street, San Francisco, CA
  94108; 415-781-5180
FLORIDA
145 S.W. 107th Ave., Miami, FL
  33174; 305-559-6715
HAWAII
1143 Bishop Street, Honolulu, HI
  96813; 808-521-2731
ILLINOIS
172 North Michigan Ave., Chicago, IL
  60601; 312-346-4228
LOUISIANA
4403 Veterans Memorial Blvd.,
  Metairie, LA 70006; 504-887-7631
MASSACHUSETTS
50 St. Paul's Ave., Jamaica Plain,
  Boston, MA 02130; 617-522-8911
Rte. 1, 885 Providence Hwy.,
  Dedham, MA 02026; 617-326-5385
MISSOURI
9804 Watson Rd., St. Louis, MO
  63126; 314-965-3512
NEW JERSEY
561 U.S. Route 1, Wick Plaza,
  Edison, NJ 08817; 908-572-1200

NEW YORK
150 East 52nd Street, New York, NY
  10022; 212-754-1110
78 Fort Place, Staten Island, NY
  10301; 718-447-5071
OHIO
2105 Ontario Street (at Prospect
  Ave.), Cleveland, OH 44115;
  216-621-9427
PENNSYLVANIA
Northeast Shopping Center, 9171-A
  Roosevelt Blvd. (between Grant Ave.
  & Welsh Rd.), Philadelphia, PA
  19114; 610-277-7728
SOUTH CAROLINA
243 King Street, Charleston, SC
  29401; 803-577-0175
TENNESSEE
4811 Poplar Ave., Memphis, TN
  38117 901-761-2987
TEXAS
114 Main Plaza, San Antonio, TX
  78205; 210-224-8101
VIRGINIA
1025 King Street, Alexandria, VA
  22314; 703-549-3806

CANADA
3022 Dufferin Street, Toronto, Ontario,
  Canada M6B 3T5; 416-781-9131